MOON FESTIVAL

中秋節

楊青
張中元

MOON FESTIVAL

by Ching Yeung Russell
Illustrations by Christopher Zhong-Yuan Zhang

BOYDS MILLS PRESS

Special thanks to my husband, Phillip Russell,
and to my editor, Karen Klockner.
—C.Y.R.

AUTHOR'S NOTE

Moon Festival, also called Mid-Autumn Festival, is celebrated on August 15 of the lunar calendar, usually in September of the western calendar. For the Chinese, it is one of the most important days of the year, other than Chinese New Year.
The moon is full, round, and brilliant—a symbol of reunion.
Everyone eats moon cakes, a special treat made for the festival.
Children play with paper lanterns shaped like animals, fish, and fruit.
Family members try their best to be home for a reunion meal, and people who are abroad feel especially homesick. Women worship the moon, where the legendary beauty Chang O lives, and ask her for a blessing on the whole family.

Published by Caroline House
Boyds Mills Press, Inc.
A Highlights Company
815 Church Street
Honesdale, Pennsylvania 18431
Printed in Mexico

Publisher Cataloging-in-Publication Data
Russell, Ching Yeung.
Moon festival / by Ching Yeung Russell ; illustrations by Christopher Zhong-Yuan Zhang.—1st ed.
[32]p. : col.ill. ; cm.
Summary : This story of children celebrating the traditional autumn Moon Festival is based on the author's memories of her childhood in China.
ISBN 1-56397-596-3
1. China—Social life and customs—Children's literature. [1. China—social life and customs—Fiction.] I. Zhang, Christopher Zhong-Yuan, ill. II. Title.
[E]—dc20 1997 AC CIP

Library of Congress Catalog Card Number 97-70583

First edition, 1997
Calligraphy by Wendy Cheng
Book design by Amy Drinker, Aster Designs
The text of this book is set in 18-point Post Antiqua.
The illustrations are done in oils.
10 9 8 7 6 5 4 3 2 1

To my parents—
Ming-Kee Yeung and Chui-Bing Chan—
and to my brother and sisters—
Patrick Yeung, Lily Kam, Rita Nishimura,
for the missing years.
—C.Y.R.

To my daughter, Xing Xin.
—C.Z.Z.

Long before the day of Moon Festival,
the whole downtown smells of cakes baking
as bakeries in town are brightened up
with golden brown moon cakes
filled with bean paste
and salty duck egg yolks
or nuts.

中秋月餅

My cousins and I
walk back and forth
in front of the stores
about a hundred times,
just sniffing
and sniffing.

茂盛
中秋月餅
中秋

The biggest bakery, Kun Hing,
displays a huge, colorful painting
of the mythical beauty, Chang O,
holding her rabbit
and rising
toward the moon.

Townspeople often stop
and admire the painting,
for Chang O
looks as if she is dancing
in the clouds,
throwing kisses
with her long, colorful cloth belts.
I wish that someday
I could rise to the moon
and pay a visit to Chang O
in the palace of the moon.

嫦娥奔月

Stores hang
colorful paper lanterns.
They are shaped like fish,
star fruits, and rabbits,
waving to us
in the autumn breeze.

We make
our own lanterns,
cut from pieces
of colorful waxed paper.
We fold them and paste them
with smashed, freshly cooked rice.
Pretty soon our lanterns
are finished–
simple and plain.
But they are as bright
as the ones
hanging
in front of the stores,
waving
in the autumn breeze.

On the day of Moon Festival,
school dismisses early,
stores close early.
Everyone hurries home
for a special feast.

My uncle comes home
by steamboat
all the way from Canton

for a family reunion meal—
whole and round and full
as the moon.
For the moon is unusually
round and bright
on Moon Festival night.

Right after the reunion meal,
each family in the village
sets up a worship table
in front of their house,
lit by the silver moonlight.

I help my grandmother, Ah Pau,
bring the chicken,
roast pork, moon cakes,
taros, and fruits
to the table.

Ah Pau lights the candles and incense
and kneels in front of our worship table,
facing the moon,
facing Chang O.
For Chang O, the beauty
who lives with her rabbit
in the palace of the moon,
will listen to us
one by one.

I hear Ah Pau ask Chang O
to bless me.
I silently ask Chang O
to bless Ah Pau
with a long life
and to help reunite me
with my parents,
who live far away.

Later, I join my cousins,
about thirty of them,
all in a line,
with lanterns in our hands.
Kee, the tallest,
leads the troop.
We all sing
as loudly as we can,
to let Chang O hear us:

**The moonlight bright,
bright in my sight,
bright in the night,
night night night,
bright bright bright!**

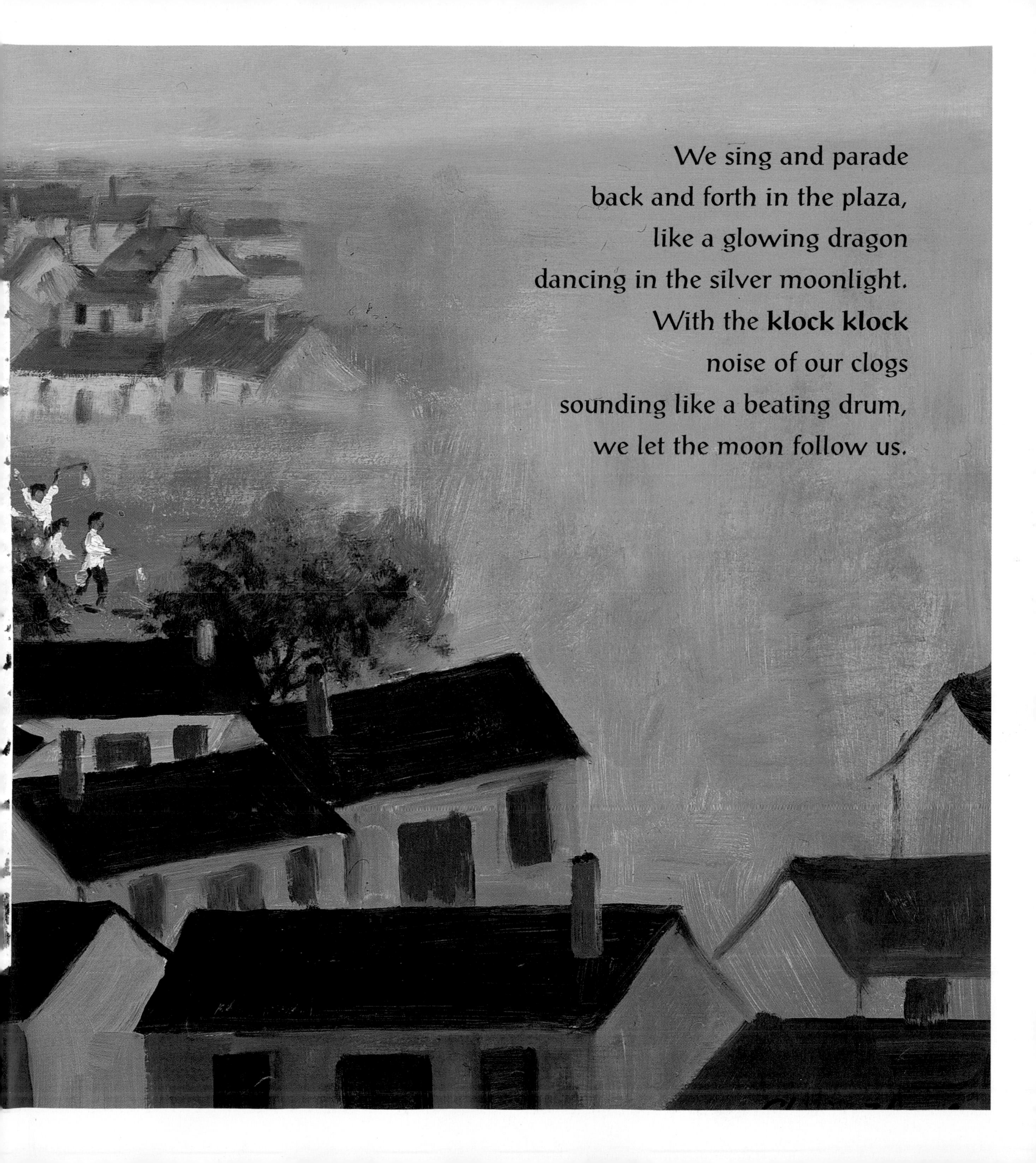

We sing and parade
back and forth in the plaza,
like a glowing dragon
dancing in the silver moonlight.
With the **klock klock**
noise of our clogs
sounding like a beating drum,
we let the moon follow us.

After worship is over,
we swarm back to our tables
for food that Chang O
has gently touched.

Ah Pau gives Kee and me
two slices of moon cake
with half a salty duck egg yolk,
two fist-sized cooked taros,
three slices of grapefruit,
one star fruit, one persimmon,
and five boiled water caltrops–
so much that I can't hold it all
in my hands.

Ah Pau helps me
make a pocket
out of my clothes
to stuff it all in!

While Ah Pau,
Uncle, and Auntie
eat and chat
with others in the plaza,
we all climb up
by the silver moonlight
to the top of Ford Hill
behind our village.
We can shake hands
with Chang O
if we just reach
way up high.

But we are so busy
eating our food,
even the ghosts around us are quiet,
and the chilly breeze is still,
listening to the way
we crack the caltrops
with our teeth!

We are so full,
we cannot eat anymore.
We throw ourselves
on the ground,
face to face with Chang O.
Kee tells ghost stories
after we give him some food.

But I do not listen
to Kee's stories.
I whisper to Chang O
and remind her of my wish,
and Chang O gives me
a broad and promising smile.

I go home
and I dream
a sweet dream—
that my mama
and baba
have returned
from far away,
just for me.

We are whole
and round
and full
as the moon
on Moon Festival night.